Bloodless

By Kelly E. Lindner

ISBN-10:0-692-78155-2
ISBN-13:978-0-692-78155-5

See all my books at KellyELindner.com.

Faces

Sometimes I think of their faces right before it happens. Though they're such different people, their expressions are always the same. Brows raised and drawn together, wrinkles centered on the forehead, mouth open, lips tensed....

They're always afraid. I always look for relief or acceptance, vainly, but it's never there.

They never want to die. They're always surprised.

Surely what they did couldn't be *that* bad.

Then I think of Billy's face before they killed him. Confused. Crying. Off-balance. Hollering about just wanting his toy cars back.

The hanging lights of the parking lot catching on the silver golf club. Them hitting him with it over and over, even though he stopped moving after the first swing.

Five different faces, bewildered and frozen, before I cut through them, each at different times over a year period.

When I think of *his* face first, I don't feel guilty.

Bloodless

June 17, 2016
Report of Terrorists on Flight Instantly Redacted
Associated Press

NEW ORLEANS—Today there was a distress call from the cellular phone of a passenger inside a plane bathroom. This eyewitness aboard flight 3427 from DFW reported seeing terrorists with bombs threatening to kill women and children if anyone thwarted their attempt to bring down the plane. Fifteen minutes later, the same passenger called to report that he was mistaken. There were no terrorists.

This was further confirmed when the plane landed and was boarded by Homeland Security. Upon searching the plane, they found no evidence of terrorists or explosives. However, one woman—covered, allegedly, in her own blood—was instantly rushed off the plane to an undisclosed hospital, where she was treated for ruptured wrists. Apparently, she had fainted and fell on a pair of sharp objects; however, none of the other passengers witnessed this bizarre accident and no sharp objects were recovered from the plane. Even the woman's husband, who was traveling with her, claimed that he "didn't see what happened." In fact, many of the passengers, some without even being asked, claimed that they "didn't see anything."

New Orleans officials say they are perplexed by this unprecedented case of mistaken terrorism, but as recently hired Orleans Parish Sheriff Robert Janus said, "It certainly could've been worse. I say we take this one as a win."

The identity of this woman was not released by officials, allegedly because she was undergoing medical treatment at press time.

Blood Traces

They told me they were taking me to the hospital, but that doesn't seem to be where I am. Even in my half-awake state, I can tell something is different. They're treating my wounds differently to begin with. Instead of the usual tugging of stitches through my skin, there's the smell of burning flesh and a strange metallic taste in my mouth. There's also this unusual sensation in my arms. They feel like they're being simultaneously emptied and filled at the same time. It doesn't make sense.

When I wake, I'm sitting in a chair in an empty room except for a long table with another person at the end of it—a black-haired man wearing a suit. Each of my wrists is handcuffed to a chair arm, and my forearms feel *heavier*. Even without the handcuffs, I'm not sure I could easily lift them in my weakened state. I look down at them to see *not* bandages but these black cloth bands stretching from wrists to elbows. When I look back to the man, I don't even try to struggle. I just ask, "What do you want?" I sound groggier than I expect.

"Kalana Janus," he says my name like it tastes bad. I'm tired of people saying my name that way.

"It's Engel, actually," I correct him. Then I have a horrible thought, and my face whitens. "Where's Tobias?"

"He's safe," he assures me with the wave of his hand. It's so dismissive I believe him.

Then he continues. "Do you have any idea how hard what you just did was to clean up?"

"*What?*" I ask.

"There were bits of terrorist all over that plane and *you*. Even after a good washing, blood leaves traces. That might've worked in Haven where your dad was the only law but *on a plane?* We had to change those flight records to subtract those two people you shredded. And dispose of their remains once we pumped the plane's septic tank. Even if your father is now the sheriff of Orleans Parish—how *convenient* by the way—you created a lot of work for us."

I start wondering who "us" is: Homeland Security? FBI? CIA? But I suspect he won't tell me, so I just ask, "Why would you clean it up?"

"Oh don't get me wrong, Mrs. *Engel.* You did a good thing. It's just how you went about it that we have a problem with."

"Is there a better way?" I ask, confused and a little irritated.

"Oh yes," he says, a strange smile spreading on his lips. "And we'd be happy to show you."

"Who's *we*?" I ask but suspect it's fruitless. He's probably trained not to answer that question. But he surprises me by saying, "A government agency," though it's vague. "But not one you've ever heard of," he adds.

Then he presses a button on a little remote control so that a door behind him swings open. Next a group of five people walk in, all dressed in black. It's a collection of men and women who are all different sizes and shapes. It's not the lineup you'd expect from the FBI or the CIA. They look like completely normal people, except a very large man on one end who is built like a wrestler.

But they all have these strange black bands stretching from their elbows to their wrists, just like what's currently on each of my arms. I glance down and wish I could peel them back and see what's underneath, but I'm still cuffed.

"Show her," the man says to the group. Simultaneously they each pull the black bands from their forearms, and there's this strange contraption built into each of their arms. It's like a metal chamber that's open on the top so whatever's inside can come out without ripping through flesh. And the skin around the metal opening is cauterized.

Their eyes darken. Then they each display the extensive bone abnormalities that are inside each of their arms in succession.

7

The wrestler-type on the end has what looks like maces inside his huge arms. The small woman next to him has something akin to sharp knitting needles. The one after that, machetes. The next one, a curved blade, and the last one, three-point blades, reminiscent of small tridents.

They're all different but all *like me*. Yet they can display what's inside without blood or pain. And their formations are not bathed in blood. They're a flawless white.

I feel my completely surprised expression draw into a smile. The man in the suit seems to like my reaction. He presses another button on his remote, and my handcuffs fall free.

Then I slowly lift my heavy wrists and pull away the black band surrounding my own strange abnormalities.

There are my knives, folded-up, bone-white and clean inside an open metal chamber that's been fused with my surrounding skin. Under my control, they slowly extend free of my arms without pain. For the first time, I see them as a gift instead of curse. They're truly beautiful.

And wielding them, I'll do beautiful things.

The Tour

Alex, the black-haired, blue-eyed agent, shows me around the strange underground facility with metal staircases, opaque skylights, florescent lights, distant ceilings and floors of concrete, while I ask too many questions.

"So you're tax-payer funded?" I ask. He doesn't answer. That means yes. "And you work with others like me?" He nods. "How many exactly?" He doesn't answer. That makes me think there're a lot more than I've seen, and I've peeked into a lot of training rooms filled with us.

"Of all the cities that you could be based in, you chose New Orleans? You must've been as disturbed by the murder rate as me."

"We're based in Washington," Alex corrects me. "There're just branches in every major city."

The significance of this stops me.

"That means there're thousands of people like me," I realize.

"Roughly," Alex allows, though doesn't add anything else.

And here I thought I was special. All those years I thought I was some one-of-a-kind super freak (well, two-of-a-kind if you count Dad), there were thousands like me out there putting their strange gifts to good use. Being productive members of society, albeit under wraps. Speaking of which....

"Is there a salary?" I have to ask. I am graduated now, and the job market is still not in great shape. Plus, I have no skills whatsoever, outside of this particularly "hard" skill I suppose.

This question makes Agent Alex laugh. There's a strange sparkle in his eyes as he nods at me.

"You'll be well compensated if you decide to join us," he tells me. The sparkle is so familiar. I start to realize that it's been there since he started this conversation while I was in handcuffs. I think it's the way that—

Uh oh. I try to diffuse this upsetting epiphany as soon as possible with mention of my husband.

"Where's Tobias?" I ask him, with a little too much chill in my voice.

"He's in our rec room," he tells me, leading the way, his eyes more guarded now. "This way."

He leads me to a room so huge it makes Tobias (skinny but muscular at 6 ft. 3 in.) look small. It's filled with pool tables, foosball tables, clear refrigerators filled with beer and 120-inch TVs blaring sports.

Tobias is playing foosball with his straw-colored hair messy (like he's just woken up from a nap), while drinking a beer, not looking the least bit concerned about anything. I take that as a sign that they've treated him well, but it annoys me a little to see him so comfortable and relaxed. I could've been with *anyone*, *anywhere* and they could've been doing *anything* to me. I had no clue where I was, and he's *here*?

"Having a good time?" I ask, a sting to my voice.

Tobias's back tenses in reaction to my voice and inadvertently hits one of the foosballs so hard it bounces out of the table.

Then he stares at me, looks me up and down, green eyes stopping at my wrists.

"What'd they do to you?" he asks, voice bathed in concern, grabbing my wrist and pulling free the black band. The flesh is still a bit pink where it meets the metal, but for the most part it's an improvement, and he seems to know this instantly. He smiles and, I melt despite myself. I'm no longer angry, even though I want to be.

I still can't help but ask, "Where *were* you?"

"Oh he didn't go quietly," Alex comes to his defense with a laugh. "We had to tranq him a few times." Then he gestures at his left arm.

I pull up his sleeve before Tobias can stop me. It's filled

with bruise-surrounded punctures.

"Was that really necessary?" I ask Alex, feeling my rage begin to build. Tobias is the kindest, calmest person I've ever met. There's no way that—

"Oh you didn't see him," Alex says.

What?

"I didn't like that they took you away," Tobias admits, shyly. "I got a little...*scary.*"

Scary? *Tobias?* "I can't even imagine that," I admit, unable to suppress a laugh.

"We even X-rayed his arms once we got him under," Alex says. "He made us wonder."

Wow.

"Well, I guess I can't be mad at you then," I admit.

"I'm still mad," he lets us both know, eyes focused on Alex. "I'm just too drugged up to show it right now," he says, but his voice does have a certain fierceness I'm not used to hearing.

I take his beer and place it away from him. I don't know why he thought that was a good idea, but I suspect he's not himself right now.

Alex clears his throat and changes the subject. "Anyway, sorry about the general roughness that lead to that enhancement," he says, nodding at my wrists. "Your people have some issues with rage, so putting you under without explanation when a gift is particularly life threatening, like yours, has become our standard procedure. It's the safest thing for everyone."

Him referring to them as "my people" makes me realize he must not be one of us.

"And we've never had someone who wasn't happy with the surgery once they saw what it did."

"Still seems like you could've explained *something* before taking action. Or asked permission to cut into someone's body," Tobias says, his anger becoming more and more apparent, while mine has actually cooled. I'm starting to fear that he's the one who might erupt.

I put my hand on his shoulder, hoping it'll let him know that I'm okay, and he doesn't need to worry. He feels me and puts his arms around my shoulders protectively. It seems to make him feel a little better.

But Alex laughs at his logical suggestion. "You'd be surprised by how often *that* doesn't work," he says.

I get it. I don't agree with forced surgery even if it is for someone's own good, but I do know that with someone like me, there really aren't a lot of options. It's possible I'd tear them all apart before they got near me with a scalpel, even if I agreed to it. Tobias has to realize that deep down. He's just mad. And I don't blame him.

But then Alex says something that spins my head. "Your father for instance, rejected this idea when we tried the 'just talking' method a while back," he says. "And put a few of our agents in the hospital when he boiled over. He's actually the reason we implemented the new policy," he says, with an awkward laugh.

"My father *hurt* some of you?" My father *knows* about these people?

"Hey we know what we signed up for," Alex reassures me. "You poke enough bears you're going to get maimed eventually."

Maimed?

He can read the disgust on my face, so he clears his throat and moves on.

"You're welcome to invite him back if you want, though," he says. "He's really...I mean...he's uniquely..."

"Strong," I say for him. It is quite amazing how un-proportionate his strength is to his compact, 5 ft. 10 in. form. I too possess a lot more strength than my small, 5 ft. 3 in. form suggests, but his is really something uncanny.

"I'll ask him," I say, trying to control my expression, but

my tight smile seems to scream, "*Yeah right.*"

If he's said no to them already and beat some of them bloody, he's not interested. And he's not one to change his mind easily.

But I really don't know if *I'm* interested. The fact that my father isn't, makes me feel like there's something even darker about this operation than I already feel. This puts me off a bit.

"And what if *I'm* not interested?" I ask.

Alex's face falls a little.

"We'd understand," he says, looking down at his feet and shuffling them. "We're just happy we got you that surgery before you eventually died from your gift. When your vectors came out, they made one of the bigger messes we've seen."

That's certainly true.

"Well, I am thankful for that," I say. "Though I don't really agree with the way you went about it."

There has to be a better way. Surely they could get someone like me to show off the benefits of the surgery before they jumped into it. I realize they probably do that in some cases. But in mine? I was probably dying again. I suspect I've almost died just about every time they've come out.

Then a question that I haven't asked yet, astounds me. One

I should've asked first.

"What am I?"

Alex looks surprised by the question and then looks down, which lets me know instantly that he doesn't know. "We're really not sure," he admits. "We have a few theories. But I think we're only going to find out by working together."

When he says this last part, he looks into my eyes, hopefully, but I just don't know.

"I'll think about it," I say, though my voice isn't convinced I will.

Alex hands me a business card. It has "Alex Michaels" and a phone number on it, but the company is merely listed as "Red's Carpets" with no address or website.

"Well, if you—or your farther—decide you want to join the fight against demons one day, give us a call."

"*Demons*?" I ask. "You mean *bad people*?"

"Sure," Alex says before he walks out of the rec room, hands in his pockets. "The way out is behind you."

Tobias and I turn to see a door clearly marked "Exit" that opens to a concrete and steel stairwell.

It eventually lets out to some non-descript alley off Bourbon Street. I'm convinced I couldn't find this place again if I wanted to.

Reluctance

Tobias and I discuss the pros and cons of joining this strange secret society while unpacking our stuff at our new apartment on Canal Street.

My dad moved into a house a month before we flew down and was nice enough to put all our stuff into his moving truck and use our spare key to drop it off here for us. All we have to do is unpack it and assemble all the furniture we bought from IKEA in Texas.

"I think it wouldn't hurt to be with your own kind," Tobias surprises me by saying, as he tears open a large box and starts stacking several planks of beige wood that will eventually be a dresser. "Even though you'd have to work with *that Alex.*"

I can't pretend I don't know what that tone in his voice means. I noticed Alex's lingering looks too.

"But what if that place isn't what is seems?" I ask, pulling clothes out of a box and putting them on hangers.

"Well, you won't know until you try it."

I bring up the strange encounter pretty quickly during dinner at Dad's new, blue double-shotgun house in the French Quarter, that night.

In fact, Dad is just finished spooning homemade mashed potatoes onto his plate when I say it.

"I got approached by...Red's Carpets today," I say, watching his expression carefully.

Clank.

"I knew that ambulance didn't look right," he says, his voice shaking with anger. "What did they do to you?"

His brown eyes start to darken. Is he about to go off? I'm almost afraid to show him.

Dad is muscular but compact at only 5 ft. 10 in. And his strength is inhuman. When he was younger and not a policeman yet, two large men tried to jump him when he walked away from an ATM. He beat them both into crying, bloody messes. They looked like they had been beaten with a police baton, but no weapon was ever found. That was the first time Dad's bone formations came out. They look like billy clubs.

"Tobias, can you give us a minute?" I try to say in an even voice, but it comes out nervous.

"I'm not going to hurt Tobias," he spits at me. "Show. Me."

Slowly, I roll up one of my sleeves, watching him carefully as I do. Despite what he says, I'm afraid I'm going to have to diffuse him in a minute.

When he sees the metal chambers fused into the surrounding pink skin that now contain my vectors, he sighs so hard I bet it hurts. Then he looks away and starts eating, like he can't stomach looking at my enhancements, but eating is somehow still possible.

I pull my sleeve back down.

"I can't believe they did that to you without permission," he says, looking at his plate instead of me, struggling to keep his temper in check.

"I can't either," I say sincerely, "But at least I won't *almost die* every time they come out. It's different for you."

Now he meets my eyes, looking especially irritated.

"What are you saying? That I should do it too?" he snaps. *I wasn't saying that at all.* It makes me wonder if he subconsciously wants the surgery. "Because they tried. I respectfully declined."

I'm not sure the men he put in the hospital and *maimed* for trying to help him deserve to be referred to with such sarcasm, but I keep my mouth shut. It isn't the time to argue about this with him; he's still shaking with anger.

I need to give him a minute (and Tobias looks extremely uncomfortable with his obvious anger), so I somewhat change the subject.

"The guy who tried to recruit me, Alex, he said the strangest thing before we left."

"I'm sure *that guy* said nothing but strange things."

So it *was* Alex who tried to recruit my dad as well. Interesting. But I ignore his unwillingness to move the conversation forward by answering the question he didn't ask.

"He said if we ever decide to join the fight against demons, we should give him a call. Isn't that weird?"

My dad's jaw tightens, and he stops eating. Uncomfortable is not a common look for him.

I'm almost afraid to ask. "What?"

"Tobias," he says. "Maybe you *should* give us a minute," he says, eyeing his plate uncomfortably.

Tobias picks up his plate and leaves the room without objection.

This isn't going to be good. He knows Tobias and I are married. I'm probably going to tell him anything he tells me anyway, but it's like he can't stomach saying whatever he's about to say out loud, in front of anyone but me.

And it takes him a while to start. It's like he's not even very comfortable telling me.

"I'm not particularly proud of this story, so try not to judge me," he says.

"Judge you? I killed five of my high school classmates."
Dad nods and begins, but after, yet another, long pause. "When I
first started as a sheriff in Haven, I'd black out like you used to. But
one night, it was particularly bad. I don't remember anything
leading up to when the switch was flipped. I don't remember
leaving work that evening. I don't remember getting out of my
patrol car.

"What I do remember is coming to in an alley covered in
black blood that smelled like fish, next to this *creature*.

"It wasn't human, and it wasn't like any animal I had ever
seen. It had *tentacles*. It looked just like an alien you would see in
some monster movie, and I had torn it to pieces, with no memory
of anything about it.

"That's when I met Alex. He came to retrieve the body with
some of his people, and that's when he told me what it was. And he
said that our kind were put on this Earth to fight them. That's
when he tried to bring me in, and I fought. That part I remember.

"But before that, I lost three hours. I could've done
anything. I could've hurt a*nyone*."

"I really doubt that," I tell him with total confidence. I
know the feeling well. I used to think I could hurt innocent people

if they got in my way, but I've learned quickly that my wrath is only reserved for murderers. Though I guess it's different if those innocent people are trying to persuade you into body altering surgery.

The only people I've shredded have been devoid of humanity, or at least I thought. Apparently there's something even more devoid of humanity walking around in the form of actual demons.

"Why haven't you told me about this before?" I ask him.

"I have only ever encountered *one*," he says with a shrug. "And I don't even remember it. I didn't think they were very common."

"Apparently they are *here*," I say, meaning New Orleans.

Then I'm quiet, and Dad knows exactly what I'm thinking.

"You're going to join them aren't you?" he asks, but there's no question in his voice. And he sounds disappointed. I don't understand why.

"What if Alex is right? What if we were put on this Earth to fight them? There has to be some reason. And can you imagine a better one than that?"

He's quiet. I take it to mean he can't.

"I can't turn my back on a mission like that," I realize as I say it. "Plus, they say there's a salary. I'd like to be something more in my life than a barista."

Then I call Tobias back in and finally start to eat. The rest of the meal is spent in silence.

I don't talk about it again until FaceTime with Morgan, my best friend who still lives in Haven (and married Eddie Sherman, from high school. Eddie was nice enough, though not who I pictured her with. But to be fair, I never got to know him too well, since he's afraid of me. Eddie is one of the only living civilians, besides Tobias and Morgan, who's actually seen firsthand what I'm capable of.)

After I tell her the whole spiel, while she's mildly distracted by her 2-year-old, Mellie, I ask her what she thinks. (Yes, she has a two-year-old already. Her teen pregnancy was quite the scandal back in the day.)

Before she can answer, Mellie grabs a handful of her mom's flawless blonde hair and pulls. Morgan gently removes the clump of hair from the toddler's grasp.

"You've never been much of a joiner," she reminds me with a laugh in her soft, musical voice. Everything about Morgan is gentle and soft.

"Maybe I'm looking to change that," I shrug. I'm not sure it's true, but I'm not sure it's not true either, which is new.

Morgan smiles, pink lips against the perfect cream of her skin. She's still just *too* pretty. It's almost nauseating.

"Well, then I think you should try it," she says.

After we hang up, I examine myself in my vanity mirror. (Tobias is in our new living room building an entertainment center.) Morgan always makes me feel insecure about the way I look. My hair is dirty blonde when hers is flawless. My eyes are that dark brown (like Dad's), when hers are that bright blue I've always envied. But it's more than that this time.

When I look at myself in the mirror, I wonder, "Can I be a joiner?"

I'm really not so sure. I've always done things my own way. But there's something nice about a group of people who are just like me. I didn't think I'd ever find such a thing. I can't help smiling at myself hopefully in the mirror.

Training

I dial the number for Red's Carpets, and an older man with a hoarse voice answers the phone, "Red's Carpets."

"Hello...I'd like to speak to Alex," I say awkwardly. I expected Alex to answer the phone.

"He'll call you back in five minutes," he says before he hangs up.

In a few minutes, my cell phone rings from a restricted number.

"Hello?"

"Hi there," says Alex's silky, confident voice. "I was getting worried you wouldn't call."

"Well, don't get *too* excited," I say. "I'm still undecided, but I'd like to check it out."

"Sounds reasonable," he says, sounding a little disappointed.

"And...my dad would like to come along too, just to observe."

There's a long pause, before he asks, "Is he *sure*?"

"He's just coming along as my protector for the time being."

At this he laughs. "You don't need protection from us," he

claims. "One, we wouldn't even try to hurt you and two, I'm pretty sure we couldn't."

Surely he's flattering me. From what I saw, I'm sure he's got someone more powerful in there than me.

Dad and I drive to the address Alex gave me, and we're surprised to pull up in front of a store with floor to ceiling windows that's filled with shelves and shelves of rolled up, vintage carpets. The big, red letters of the sign do indeed read "Red's Carpets."

Behind the counter, sitting on stool, leaning against the wall, *asleep* is an elder man with a name tag that reads "Red."

I clear my throat, and he opens his eyes, looking pissed.

"Welcome to Red's Carpets," he says, in a bored, gruff voice. It's the same voice that answered the phone when I called Alex.

"Do you actually *sell* carpets?" I can't keep myself from asking. My father gives me a warning look.

"Of course," he says, looking annoyed. "But we only accept cash."

Then he closes his eyes again.

Wow. So they're cash only with shitty customer service. I guess this secret government agency doesn't want this cover to do a lot of real business. From the card Alex gave me, it seems they don't even seem to have a website or an email. Just a phone number. There *is* a '50s phone on the counter, but there's no way that thing has caller ID capability. How did he get my cell number to Alex from *that* phone so he could call me back?

"We're here to see Alex Michaels," Dad speaks up. Red's eyes land on him for the first time, and he's amazed.

"Why, Sheriff," he says. "I didn't notice that was *you*. You look taller on TV."

Dad grunts. This isn't the first time someone's said this to him. He has such a commanding presence that people are often shocked by his height when they see him in person.

Red presses a button behind the counter, and the brick wall behind him slides open. "Have fun," he says, with a sardonic smile.

We walk through the opening into a stairwell, where a metal staircase folds down for several floors. This part looks familiar.

After we descend the staircase we walk out into one of the cavernous rooms I remember, and Alex is standing in the center of it, wearing his suit, smiling at us.

"Welcome to Red's Carpets," he says.

After my dad receives the same tour I had the other day and does a lot of emotionless grunts and "uh huhs," we're each presented with our very own black body suit exactly in our size.

"I'm not wearing that leotard," my dad says dismissively.

"If you want to be in the training room with Kalana, you'll have to. It's a bit intense, and loose clothing tends to get...*caught on stuff*."

I'm now a little worried about what this training room entails.

Alex also warns me that I'll have to remove my necklace before we enter, though I don't know how he noticed it tucked inside my shirt.

Billy, Tobias's brother, gave me this necklace. Billy, who I killed five boys from my school to avenge.

It's a silver charm of an angel stabbing some kind of reptilian demon with a staff. Billy said he found it in the street one night, and it reminded him of me.

It's regrettable, but I understand.

I unhook it and reluctantly hand it over.

Alex senses that it's important to me.

"I'll take good care of it, I promise," he says.

When the massive metal doors slide open, it's the size of an airplane hangar, and at the very center is what I assume is an actual live demon fighting five people just like us, all dressed in the black body suits that stretch from wrists to ankles (just like what we've recently changed into). And they seem to be having a bit of trouble defeating it.

It looks just like what my father described, an alien from a monster movie with a large head, thick shoulders that surround a hidden neck and tentacles surrounding each of its arms that it uses to grab whoever attacks it and throw he/she about 20 feet.

My eyes flash to my dad. He took down one of these by himself?

He can see the question in my eyes and just shrugs.

"You're welcome to jump in," Alex says from behind us. "We have no doubts about the evilness of these creatures. We grabbed this one, unfortunately, after it had eaten a three-year-old boy. We brought it in for training purposes, because this one is especially large."

"*Eaten*?" I repeat angrily. I sense that my eyes have turned black. When I look at my dad, his have done the same.

After we push past the sweating, panting trainees surrounding the creature, I send my vectors straight to the strange shoulder-like bone surrounding its neck. Of course, it throws tentacles at me, but I cut through them all so they spray black blood before falling to the ground in a black, bloody mess. The bone surrounding its neck is thick, but my vectors slice right through it and pry it open so it falls free to the ground in a black bloody clump. My father appears behind it while it's trying to fight me off and snaps its neck with one motion. Then the thing that five people like us couldn't take down is dead.

It's strange that we can eat after this, but everyone is hungry and exhausted, so we go straight to the cafeteria, and it turns out to be fairly easy to do after a mere handwash, despite being covered in sweat and black blood.

The cafeteria is crowded with other trainees, but we're invited to sit with the "B-Team," as they call themselves. They're the best, but it still needs to be in code. A-Team would be too obvious.

"Your vectors are really long," says Needle, a blonde woman who has long pointed sticks inside her that look like knitting needles, almost begrudgingly. "I didn't know they could be that long. I couldn't even get near that thing."

"And they're sharp," says Mace, the big guy. This man has something inside his huge, thick arms that look like maces. He and they are enormous. I'm shocked that he had any trouble taking that thing down, honestly. "Mine are better for crushing, but not so much cutting," he says.

"And you," says Trident, the tall guy with black hair and multiple piercings, whose bone formations look like tridents. (The code names are pretty straight forward, but I'm worried that mine is going to end up being something like "Fan Knives.") "You didn't even get yours out. What you got in there anyway, Sheriff?"

My dad doesn't answer, so I do it for him.

"They look like Billy Clubs," I say.

"Billy Club," Trident repeats excitedly. "That's perfect, Sheriff."

Billy Club is pretty fitting.

"But you didn't even need yours, *Billy Club*," Trident continues. "You broke his neck with your bare hands. I tried that once. Those things feel like they're made of pure concrete."

My dad is embarrassed by any recognition of his impressive strength, which is silly, but *him*. Modest to the end.

"Well, Kalana made it easy," he says after clearing his throat. "Ripping apart that boney part that protected its neck. My part was easy."

So not true, and they sense it, but all nod like they agree.

32

Arguing with my Dad is just. Well. Few do it.

"Your name is Kalana?" asks Machete, the redhead who has what look like machetes in her arms, sounding disappointed. "Shit, I was gonna name you Katana, like the chick in Mortal Combat with the fan knives, but Kalana is so close to that, why bother?"

I feel a smile tug at one corner of my mouth, but I fight to resist it.

Awesome. No lame code name for me.

To keep anyone from trying to mess this up for me, I change the subject.

"So how long have you all been doing this?" I ask.

Needle: "5 years."

Mace: "12 years."

"Trident: "7 years."

Machete: "2 years."

"And you find this work...fulfilling?"

"More fulfilling than piercing and tattooing people's various body parts," Trident says. I'm not surprised he worked in a tattoo parlor once.

"It's more than that. Anytime we take down one of those things, we keep them from killing someone," Machete says.

33

"Because from what we've seen, that's mostly what they like to do."

"And none of you regret getting the surgery?" I ask, eyeing Dad. He gives me an annoyed look.

"No," Needle says. "It makes the gift pretty painless, which is nice. And it's better if we don't leave our blood at crime scenes, anyway. That always leads to trouble."

I can't help watching my dad's reaction. He doesn't seem as annoyed now and takes a thoughtful bite of his fruit salad, but that's about it.

"So do you guys have any theories about what we are?"

They all laugh and look at Mace, but I don't know why.

"I do," Mace says shyly.

I nod to him, waiting.

He blushes a little before he speaks. "Well, they're demons, right?" he asks. "And we fight them. I don't see how that doesn't make us angels."

I don't laugh at that. It's not the first time I've been called such a thing, though we certainly don't look like the angels of various religious depictions, unless you start sliding more toward *Dante's Inferno*.

"But you probably think that's funny."

"No," I say. "I don't. I do feel a little sorry for the world if

34

I'm an angel though."

Dad gives me a confused look, but he's biased.

"You shouldn't," Needle says. "Didn't you just save a whole plane full of people from some terrorists? They didn't say in the news who it was, but you just moved here, right?"

I look to Dad for some silent advice. He gives me a level look that tells me to neither confirm nor deny that statement.

"I've definitely saved some people in the past," I say cryptically. "But when I first started out, I was just punishing people that had already killed someone. Seems pretty out of bounds."

"Not for us," Machete says. "I think we've been put here for that more than anything else—to judge and punish the wicked. I think that's our job. If it wasn't, we would be human, which we're clearly not."

I can't argue with that. Dad's face relaxes too. I suspect he finds that statement as infallible and comforting as I do.

"Do you guys ever kill humans, or just demons?" I ask.

Needle swallows hard before she speaks. "We kill anything that's out of balance in a bad way," she says. "That's *killed*."

"Out of balance?"

"Everyone has a balance of good and evil: humans,

demons, whatever we are, even animals, though they're mostly all balanced, even predators since they mostly just kill to eat. Though Trident swears that his cat is evil to demonic levels," Needle says.

"All he does it bite me and pee on my stuff. And he's 30. How is that not a demon?"

Most laugh, but Needle merely cracks a smile before continuing. "They're either more good than evil, more evil than good or balanced between the two," Needle says. "When someone's out of balance and tipping toward evil, we can feel it. That's why some humans are just as bad as demons. No doubt those boys you killed were practically demon level in their evilness. (Wow. So I guess they know about that. I wonder how much.) Some demons are actually harmless, and some of...*us*...actually go bad."

She looks away when she says that last part. I sense that she's actually known someone like us that's gone bad, but doesn't want to talk about it, so I ask about the other thing that piqued my interest.

"There are *harmless* demons?"

"It doesn't happen often," Mace says. "I found her in a sewer caring for a litter of kittens that had lost their mom."

"What happened?" I ask.

"I said, 'Nope. Not killing that.' And came back and told

36

Alex," Mace says.

"Where is she now?"

"She's actually *here*. Would you like to meet her?"

The Demonic Angel

Seeing through the glass is startling. She's like a 10-foot long, three-foot thick, black cobra with hair-like tentacles sprouting from either side of her human-sized head. But her face, and stunning blue eyes, are gentle, despite the tongue that flickers between her smiling mouth.

It's odd to be in her presence. Calming. I admitted to Mace that I was afraid to see her. I feared I'd trigger and hurt her, like my father (who declined visiting altogether), but Mace assured me that no one ever triggered around her, because you can feel her goodness.

I was curious enough to chance it, and now I know exactly what he means. I *can* feel her goodness, even through the glass that separates us.

But it's more than a feeling. It's her actions. She has a whole family of baby animals that she's caring for inside her large, glass chamber. Squirrels, kittens, turtles, hedgehogs...The list goes on.

She rolls over and exposes her belly, showing many nipples that the animals can use to feed on for milk.

If she's a demon, why is she even designed that way?

"That's a good question, Kalana," says a soothing female

voice inside my head. I look around for the voice's source, but there's no one else in the room, except Mace. Then I lock eyes with the supposed demon, and she's smiling at me. Is that *her*?

"It's because all demons are actually angels," the voice says. "Demon is just the word given to a *fallen angel*."

So she's actually an angel who just happens to look demonic?

She nods. "My name is Hayyel."

"She's talking to me inside my head," I tell Mace, as I stare into her hypnotic blue eyes.

Mace looks surprised. "Well, yeah she's telepathic," he says. "But I'm the only other one she's ever spoken to, so no one else even knows that, except Alex."

No wonder he didn't mention it. I wonder why she's chosen to talk to me.

"Because like Mace, you're out of balance in a very good way," the voice says. "Just like your father."

"You know my father?" I ask.

"Not directly," the voice says. "But I see him inside your mind. I can tell he's like you. You should bring him in for a visit."

"He's afraid he'll hurt you," I say. "The last time he encountered a demon, he killed it without asking any questions...or remembering."

"I know," she says. "His body led him in doing the right thing in that instance, just as it would here."

I know she's right, but my father is going to be harder to convince. He would never risk hurting something innocent.

"Your father would never hurt me, Kalana," Hayyel says. "Neither would you. I'm safe with both of you. But no need to pressure him. He'll come when he's ready."

"Are you happy in there?" I can't help asking. The glass cage is large, but it's still a cage.

"Absolutely," she says. "I have protection, which is something I've lived without for hundreds of years. You wouldn't believe how many people would kill a large snake-like creature on sight without asking questions."

Oh I would. My dad especially hates snakes.

"And I have my babies. They bring me any strays they find. I love it here."

"I'm glad," I say before an easy, sincere smile.

"You really should meet her," I tell Dad later. "She's amazing."

"No thanks on the giant snake," he says simply.

But she seemed so confident he would visit eventually. I

wonder why.

The Fallen Angel

I'm standing in the center of an alley, in a downpour, with a man centered before me like we're about to draw for a gunfight. His face is shadowed, and he wears a trench coat with holes cut in the back to accommodate his *angel wings*.

They've folded up now, but I imagine they span several feet when they're extended. The feathers are the purest white I've ever seen. They're iridescent and shine silver.

That's when I notice the first feather fall, and then clumps and heaps of them until there're no feathers left. Just black bones in the outline of angel wings, extended.

I wake with a gasp.

Tobias wakes too.

"What's wrong?" he asks, rubbing his eyes.

I'm in our newly built bed in our New Orleans apartment on the third floor. Not standing at the center of a wet alley.

"Just a dream," I say.

But Tobias doesn't seem to buy that.

"Hopefully," he says, wrapping his arms around me. He holds me until I fall asleep without another word, but I feel his jaw tense against my forehead.

I visit Hayyel after training the next day to ask her about

the strange dream.

She's not surprised by my presence or the question. It's like she knew I was coming.

"Angels have the gift of prophecy," she tells me inside my mind.

"So *you* showed me that?" I ask.

"No," she says with a laugh. "You showed that to yourself."

So Mace's dumb theory is right? We're actually *angels*?

She nods.

But I've done such horrible things, thinking of all the blood...the death.

"Were they horrible?" she asks me. "Or were they *necessary*?"

"You'd never kill anyone," I say out loud. It's an assumption, but it feels like a pretty safe one.

"I would to protect them," she says nodding at the baby animals that share her cage. "Because that's my charge. Protecting the humans is what you're here to do."

"So who is the angel I saw?" I ask.

"They called him Scythe," she tells me.

I'm assuming because he has something that look like scythes inside his arms.

43

"Did you know him?"

"Not directly," she says sadly, "But there are a few here who did."

I want to ask Needle about Scythe during training that day. I remembered her discomfort when she was explaining the concept of being "out of balance" to me. She's the one who mentioned that sometimes people like us could be out of balance in a bad way. But training is especially vigorous. And focusing on a good opening to ask about Scythe distracts me enough to get me cut by one of the demon's tentacles, which I've never let happen before.

I wonder if they're—

My whole arm goes numb in seconds, and black starts to trace the veins in my arm.

"Stop!" Alex yells before he runs to my side and yanks my arm under his eyes, so he can examine it.

"Go see the doctor," he orders, sounding so panicked it freaks me out. I jump when he yells, "Now, Kalana!"

I sprint the whole way to the medical wing.

I've never been there before. (Alex hadn't shown it to me on the tour.) So I follow signs until I see one that merely says "doctor" and open the door.

The room is typical, but the person standing at its center

smirking at a nurse with his arms crossed, *isn't*.

He's not just some doctor. He's *my* doctor. My childhood doctor (since age 11 anyway), my adolescent doctor and my adult doctor (before I left Haven).

He's the one who would stitch me up after my bone-knives shredded my wrists every time they came out. Before I blacked out and killed murderers with no memory of it. Back when I used to do that.

He's the one who helped me but never told anyone about me, aside from Dad who is also his patient.

Dr. Menzer. Weird, sarcastic, Dr. Menzer.

When he sees me, he drops his head in guilt. I am shocked to see him.

"Hello....*Kalana*," he says, flatly.

"Dr. Menzer?" I ask, but my tone asks something more like, "What the *fuck* are you doing here?"

He sees the blackening veins in my arm, now spreading up to my shoulder, and insists I take a seat.

I crawl awkwardly onto the raised, padded hospital chair.

"We're going to need to drain the wound fast," he tells the nurse. "It's seconds from the heart."

Shit. No wonder Alex screamed at me to run here.

The nurse wheels in a machine (reminiscent of a vacuum) with clear tubes hanging off it that each end in needles. She hands one of these sharp tubes to Dr. Menzer, who, without any warning, jams the sharp needle into my wound.

I gasp in pain, but he ignores me. He's watching the veins in my arms carefully as the machine sucks out both blood and black venom quickly with a loud motor.

"I suppose you're wondering how long I've worked for this organization," he says loudly over the machine, eyes still on my arm.

I wince. The tube in my arm continues drawing out black liquid. It stings.

Dr. Menzer did move to Haven (my hometown) promptly after the incident where my dad beat two giant guys almost to death with his billy club bone vectors. To be fair, they had it coming. They were trying to jump him and take his wallet.

"You worked for them before you even became my doctor," I realize. "They sent you there to watch me and Dad."

The feeling slowly returns to my arm as the blood/venom drawing through the tube fades from black to dark red.

"Watch and *help*," he clarifies, meeting my eyes sincerely. It's a rare thing to see. It's almost uncomfortable.

"And I moved to this facility when you moved to New Orleans...so I could keep watching you."

When he says this, he meets my eyes again in a heartfelt, sincere way. It's completely out of character for him. I feel like I'm meeting the real Dr. Menzer for the first time. Someone who's not all sarcasm and snarky comments, though still mostly these things.

"Is your name even Dr. Menzer?" I tease him.

It's not kind, but I'm still getting over him jamming a needle into one of my veins without warning, not that he had much choice.

"Yes," he says, sounding offended. "Of course."

When the blood returns to a normal shade, he removes the tube and slides the strange machine to the nurse who wheels it away.

Then he cleans the wound and tapes a square bandage over it.

"It didn't get to your heart, so you'll *probably* be okay," he says, with so much emphasis on 'probably' it's not comforting. "But next time come as soon as you get stuck."

I did, but I don't argue with him. I have no intention of letting one of those demonic tentacles touch me ever again.

After he tells me I'm free to resume training, I stand and

extend my hand, which confuses him. Carefully he takes it but keeps his eyes on me, waiting for the catch.

"Nice to finally meet you, Dr. Menzer," I say, with a sincere smile that reaches my eyes.

He smiles sincerely too. It looks strange on him, but it's not *that* bad.

But the moment doesn't last long. "Well, don't get all gushy on me," he says. "Go kill some demons or something."

After my unexpected encounter with Dr. Menzer, I enter the lunch room, to find Needle sitting alone at a table eating.

I plop down next to her and get straight to it.

"I had a dream about Scythe last night," I say.

Her face falls.

She tells me everything about him in the cafeteria in a hushed voice.

He was already there when she joined. He took her "under his wing" so-to-speak.

That's when I break in with probably a very stupid question.

"Did he actually have wings?" I ask.

"No," she laughs. "That part of your dream was just a

dream. We don't have wings—us *angels*," she stresses sarcastically. "Just the bone formations and the rage blackouts."

"So what happened?" I pushed.

"Around the same time as Mace, Scythe and me found another demonic Angel like Hayyel in the sewer, except Scythe killed him. It felt wrong. He was kind. He had stray puppies he was caring for. He begged, but I didn't stop Scythe. He insisted he was a demon."

I can guess why. The way her eyes fill with a bittersweet regret when she talks about him. I think she loved him; I suspect she still does.

"He was Hayyel's mate, actually. They had gotten separated. But Mace spared her and Scythe didn't spare him. When he came back and saw her here, in her glass cage, he wanted to kill her. Said she was demon. That's what we're here to do. But Alex wouldn't let him. Said we were better than that. This didn't sit well with Scythe. He attacked Alex. Messed him up pretty good."

"What'd he do to Alex?" Alex certainly doesn't look like he's been majorly hurt in any way, though this was apparently a couple of years ago.

Needle gets uncomfortable. "You'll have to ask him."

"Anyway, then Scythe left and didn't come back. A few

months later we found the body of an old, homeless woman in the street with white feathers scattered around her. The note said, 'Things that look evil usually are.'"

"Was she evil?"

She shrugs, but the tears in her eyes make me think she doesn't buy it. "We can't tell once something is dead."

"Has it happened again?"

Her face drops. Then she reluctantly nods.

"How many times?"

"A lot over the last two years."

"And the people? Was there any indication they were actually evil outside of their...*appearance*?"

She shakes her head.

Sabre

The next morning I'm thinking about what Needle told me.

I'm also attempting to make Tobias crepes and failing miserably. It's not too hot this morning, so I have the windows open. The air smells delicious because of a nearby crawfish boil— not because of whatever I'm doing. It's discouraging.

Tobias steps in with a patient smile. Suddenly, everything is relaxed, and the food presented in the end is actually good-smelling, crepe-like and delicious. Strawberries, batter and cream cheese.

"Needle says he always dumps their bodies in an alley with a note and some white feathers."

"Sounds like a real winner," he says dismissively, pouring more coffee into my cup.

"Am I talking about this too much?" I ask, realizing that's it been a long while since we've talked about anything that just concerns Tobias.

He gives me that usual sincere, never-faked smile, matched with those bright green eyes, and I melt. I always melt.

"Your stuff is pretty important," he says. "I understand that."

"But so is your stuff," I say, though it sounds forced despite

51

my best efforts. But he doesn't mind. Tobias never minds. Tobias is the reason I get out of bed in the morning. Without him, I don't think I'd bother.

"The ER seems tame compared to your stuff," he tells me. Tobias is training to become an ER nurse. He's always loved helping people.

"But what about all my weird stuff?" I ask. "How are you taking it?"

"What? Finding out that you were an angel all along?" he says, again with that smile. "I already knew that."

Why am I dressed? But I blush, smile and try to move the conversation forward. "No, I mean all this weird stuff about the demon-fighting government organization and the angel that has gone rogue. How are you taking it?"

He shrugs, but he looks uncomfortable as he does so. "I trust you," he says. "I know you'll handle it. But I guess I am worried about this Scythe guy. It's seems like you'll come up against him eventually. And when you do, what will you do?"

"I don't know," I lie. I'll have to kill him. There's no way around it. He's killing innocent people, but I can't even stomach saying that out loud. I don't think he's evil necessarily. Just lost and doing evil things. But maybe there isn't a difference.

"Then there's Alex," Tobias adds, a strange edge to his voice that I haven't heard often.

I can't pretend not to know what he means.

"I only met him once. But the way he looks at you—"

"You don't need to worry," I assure him, because it's true.

"I know," he says, still that smile. "It's not *you* I'm worried about."

Then he thinks further. "Well, maybe it is," he says. "Don't hurt him okay? I don't blame him for finding you...*completely appealing*."

That smile again. I kiss him. I can't help it. But why should I? We're married after all.

Both we and bits of uneaten crepes end up on the floor....in a good way.

But I don't heed his warning as I should. A few days later, when I'm training with Alex one-on-one (Who knows why?), after we dispatch the actually evil demon, he does lean in and try to kiss me out of nowhere, after sharing the story of how a demon killed his father.

I was sympathetic. That was it. I wasn't signaling him. And before his overzealous lips can touch mine, I punch him in the face hard. Probably too hard.

"This is *not* a love triangle!" I snap, feeling the blackness filling my eyes. How could he even think that? I've done nothing to make him think that. "I am happily married!"

"I know that," he says, rubbing his red cheek. "You're just wonderful. I can't help it."

"You'd better help it." It's not the first time someone has called me wonderful. Tobias said that to me two years ago, and I married him.

"I love my husband *Tobias*," I tell him. It's true. There's no other truth.

"I know," he says with a sigh. "We're just so much alike."

I don't know how that could possibly be true, until he pulls back the sleeves of his body suit and shows me his arms, with the the same Frankenstein-like scars cutting longwise along each wrist that I used to have before the surgery.

"I used to be just like you," he says. "Until Scythe neutered me. He said I didn't deserve my gifts because I didn't know the difference between an angel and a demon."

I can't stop staring at the scars on his forearms. I had no idea, but his involvement in this organization makes so much more sense now.

"What were they?" I can't help asking.

"They used to call me Sabre."

"When was this?" I ask.

"About two years ago," he says. "Why?"

"They haven't grown back?"

"*What*?"

"Um. Mine were removed once, but they grew back," I tell him, shocked that he doesn't already know this. "Dr. Menzer didn't tell you?"

I can tell from his expression that he didn't, and I have to know why.

Our next stop is Dr. Menzer.

"Why didn't you tell Alex that his bone formations can grow back?" I ask as soon as we enter.

Dr. Menzer had smiled when he saw me, only to have it drop after my question. "Hello, Kalana. Always a pleasure," he says with his character-defining sarcasm. Then he sighs very audibly before he says, "Because it's only happened in half the removal cases I've seen. I didn't want to get your hopes up."

"Oh," Alex says with disappointment.

"So I made it classified," Dr. Menzer adds.

This startles Alex. "*Classified*? I'm your *boss*."

"As far as you know," Dr. Menzer says, winking at him. Then he changes the subject. "So, Kalana. I can't help but notice that your father hasn't come in for his physical this year."

"I don't think he considers you his doctor anymore," I say.

"I don't care," he snaps seriously. Then he walks out of the room after saying, "I have patients," over his shoulder.

Alex looks around and notices no one else in the hospital wing. "*Where?*" he demands, but he's gone.

I would be more frustrated if I didn't know him so well.

"What the hell did he mean by *that*?" Alex demands as we start our walk back to the training wing.

"He's been my doctor half my life, and I had no idea he worked for your organization," I say. "If he doesn't want you to know something, you won't, but he's not above making snarky comments about it."

"So he's somehow my superior, and I have no idea," Alex says. "Is that what you're saying?"

"Or he's messing with your head for fun," I shrug.

It really could be either. But I suspect Dr. Menzer is high up in this organization since all he had to do to transfer was, apparently, ask.

"Well, thank you *so much* for bringing *that guy* here with you."

"You're welcome," I say with a snarky smile. I'm still angry at him for the attempted kiss.

When I get home that evening, I tell Tobias about Dr. Menzer and what Alex tried to do.

He's not thrilled.

"I knew that was coming," he says, running his hands through his straw-colored hair, nervously. "What did you do?"

"Punched him in the face."

Half of his face pulls into a smile. "How hard?"

"Too hard," I admit. He told me not to be too hard on him.

But the smile spreads to both sides of his face.

"Good," he says, before giving me a very welcome kiss.

Scythe

Eventually my father steps back from Red's Carpets and leaves it to me, feeling satisfied that it's safe enough and they're not bad people. Plus, he can only take so long a sabbatical from being the sheriff of Orleans Parish. It's kind of an important position, since New Orleans happens to have the highest murder rate in the nation, even with a branch of *us* in our secret underground facility.

"Plus, I'm sure a bunch of youngsters don't want some old guy cramping their style," he says.

I try to make him realize how silly that is. "They want you in this fight," I tell him. "You're clearly the strongest of us they've ever seen."

He just huffs, and that's it. Conversation over. Modest to the end.

But having Red's connected with the sheriff turns out to be helpful.

Though Red's is secretly tapped into the police station's server and knows the second something's reported, my father has a talent for pretty accurate hunches before crimes happen. It's part of the reason he became a cop, aside from the inhuman strength. He just knows when something's fishy.

"I saw *this guy* stalking down an alley in the Lower Ninth

58

Ward," he calls to tell me one night. "He looked a little sketchy, but I lost track of him. I thought maybe a group of you could look around for him on foot."

"Sure," I say. "What did he look like?"

I can't help passing the description onto Needle, because I have a hunch too.

Six foot 5, spiked blonde hair, brown trench coat and an angelic face. (Yes, my dad actually allowed himself to use such a corny word, so it must be true.) I also know why he called me instead of following this guy on foot himself. He has a feeling this alley stalker isn't human, and he doesn't trust himself not to beat him to death in front of his partner. He hopes a group of us will take care of him under the radar, without blacking out. Plus, he suspects, as I do, that it's actually one of *us*, which means he would be best handled by our new allies.

"Does that sound like Scythe?" I ask Needle immediately after I describe him.

Needle nods. Reluctantly. "He hasn't been spotted in months," she says. "So be ready for a trap."

We are. We bring everyone, except Alex, of course, and he's waiting for us in an alley, not too far from the cross streets my father mentioned.

It's like he suspects the sheriff is tipping us off.

When the five of us approach him (Needle, Mace, Trident, Machete and I), he's kneeling on some second-story balcony, with something large, motionless and shadowed lying at his feet.

Once we stand directly beneath him, he throws it over the railing.

It hits the asphalt with a splat. It is a very heavy, very dead obese man, though he's dressed so casually in shorts, a fanny pack and a button-down shirt with turkey legs drawn all over it, I doubt he's any kind of criminal.

I can't help but watch Needle's reaction first, disappointment overshadowing a quiet, but vain, hope. The rest of us are just disgusted and angry. I myself am starting to boil over, which isn't good.

Needle speaks first. "Why are you doing this, Scythe?" she asks, voice shaking.

"I'm making a point," Scythe says. His voice is strange. Almost musical in its pleasantness. It's odd to hear such a voice utter such unpleasant things. "This is what we're here to do," he says. "Clean up garbage, human and demon alike. And this is human garbage," he says, jamming a finger toward the unfortunately dead man before us.

Though one thing Needle told me: we can't feel whether someone is out of balance in a bad way after death. We can only make assumptions based on what we see.

"What did he do to earn your judgement?" Needle asks. The naked hope in her voice pains me. She desperately wants him to tell us that this man was evil, that he had murdered or attempted to murder, because that is the only right answer for us. But I know better. I know what he's about to say, and if he says it, my eyes will blacken, and I will send a vector straight to his throat.

I've been moving closer every time his eyes aren't on me. My vectors are long. I can almost reach him from here. I just need to sneak one more step.

"The greediest of the seven deadly sins," he says. "Gluttony."

There's a collective groan of disgust. I take my last step toward him and send my vector to his throat.

But it just slices air. He jumps back just fast enough to avoid it.

"Whoa-hoooh!" he yells before he moves as far away from my now extended vectors as he can, then leans over the railing, staring down at me in awe.

"So you must be the new one," he says. "I've never seen

61

vectors that long."

I'm heaving in anger. I've lost the element of surprise. He won't let me near his fragile, exposed throat now, but I move toward him anyway hoping he'll slip up.

But he keeps his distance perfectly. Walks backwards as he continues to talk to me.

"You're an especially angry one," he says, probably disturbed by the complete blackness of my eyes, while his have remained a watery blue. "How valuable you'll be if I make you see the light too."

"I tried with this one," he says, pointing down at Needle, who's standing directly beneath him. "But she wouldn't yield to me."

That's when he sends one of his vectors down to Needle so fast, that in a half of a second, she's picked off her feet with a scythe-like bone sticking through her heart from behind.

Then he drops her and disappears up onto the roof, while we all scream.

She's buried in one of those huge French Quarter graveyards. Among the rows of stone mausoleums and somber jazz music, Needle's friends, family and us, posing as her work colleagues from Red's Carpets, say goodbye. (The only one who doesn't pretend to be a colleague is Dad, since he's very visible as the sheriff of Orleans Parish.) Needle's mother is honored and confused by his presence. He apologizes for not being able to save her. He says he was hot on the guy's trail but lost him and promises he'll get him. She just nods numbly.

Of course, it was us who failed to save her. Not him. It annoys me that he's taking credit for our failure. But that's just him.

It turns out Needle's name was Jennifer. And aside from her parents who are still living, because she was only 36, she has a two-year-old daughter, Sabrina.

The child's father isn't at the funeral, but I have a feeling I know who he is, considering the timing. Needle and Scythe were together about two years ago.

But even if Scythe isn't the father, Sabrina is one of us, since her mother was. It tends to run in families. It did with Dad and me.

During the ceremony, I steal glances at her forearms, but the skin there is smooth and unbroken.

They haven't come out yet. Her grandmother and grandfather are holding her between them affectionately. I suspect she's been surrounded by family and goodness her whole life (except her absent father, of course). Good. Maybe her vectors will never have to come out.

But I know it's a vain hope. This world is so full of unnecessary violence.

Suddenly, the rose-covered casket is shadowed by a tall figure standing atop of one of the mausoleums.

I glance up in time to see Scythe just before he sends his vector so that it cuts perfectly into the hood of Sabrina's jacket and yanks her away from the loving arms of her grandparents like a fish on a line. Then there's a moment of surprised gasps where she joins him on top of the stone structure, before they're gone.

They've most likely gone down the other side, and he's running on foot while carrying her. Hopefully that means he can't run as fast. Everyone from Red's Carpets plus Tobias gives chase without a word. Dad radios for backup while joining us.

"He's gonna kill her," Machete whispers too loudly in my ear. Everyone hears.

"There wasn't any blood," I say. "I think he's just *taking* her."

"That *bastard*," Machete hisses in a loud whisper. "He thinks he has a right to her after *killing* her mother, who LOVED

HIM!"

I shake my head. I don't know what to say.

We run straight to the entrance first and Dad, Machete, Tobias and I continue down the road looking for some kind of trail. Tobias has no trouble keeping up with us despite that he isn't on the super-strength team. He ran track in high school. He participated in just about every sport in high school.

"We're not gonna find anything," Machete tells us angrily as we watch the grounds carefully while keeping a steady pace. "Aside from Scythe, we used to call him *stealthy*."

The others turn back to the cemetery to make sure he's not hiding somewhere in there. Thirty minutes later we meet back up at the entrance with no glimpse of him or any trail, just like Machete predicted.

Eventually we have to tell the grieving friends and family something. It's the truth. The father kidnapped his own child, but we don't think he intends to hurt her. We don't mention that this is the same person who killed Needle.

Backup arrives and questions everyone. Dad conducts the situation like he would any other. It doesn't seem suspicious except for the large knives on a chain he used to hook and drag off the 2-year-old. All the policemen not in-the-know (which is everyone except Dad) are harping on that, though Dad is noticeably dismissing it as a "new gang weapon" he's recently seen.

Dad assures Jennifer's mother that he will find Sabrina and return her.

Once the funeral party is done with answering questions—and they and the cops and Dad disperse—only Machete, Mace, Trident, Alex, Tobias and I remain.

"Why did he take her?" Mace demands once everyone else is out of earshot.

Alex glances down at his arms, even though they're covered by sleeves.

"He wants to convert her to *his* idea of justice."

The remaining workday is depressing to say the least. We don't train. We just sit around the table in our situation room and strain to figure out where he might've taken her and what he may do to her.

Alex seems to have the most insight into the inner workings of Scythe's mind, now that Needle is gone.

"He'll train her," he says.

"She's 2," Machete objects, but she's ignored.

"He has to have a training room somewhere underground.

It's probably already stocked though, so he won't be buying anything for it anytime soon. Unless he has to replace something. I'll watch purchases in the city."

"And we'll watch the alleys," Machete says. "The bad ones. See if he shows up to take out any *human garbage*."

That night we patrol all the bad alleys in teams. Mace is with Trident, and Machete is with me.

She doesn't say much. She's too sad, I suspect. I am as well, but obviously didn't know Jennifer as well.

We're trying to be stealthy, but the silence is uncomfortable.

"Why would Scythe kill her?" I ask the question that's been gnawing at me all day. "Didn't he love her?"

"That's why he was so offended that she didn't see things his way, I suspect. He was a very 'my way or the highway' kind of guy."

"But he had to know that Needle was, in no way, *evil*."

"Neither was that poor overweight bastard he killed. He can't handle the power we have. It's warped his mind. We need to kill him before he kills someone else."

I do want to kill him. The way he killed someone who loved

him because she wouldn't walk his insane path. And now he has the audacity to steal their daughter from her healthy and sheltered upbringing.

"Are you about to erupt?" Machete's voice breaks into my thoughts. My eyes have certainly darkened. "Because I'd like to be elsewhere," she says, stepping away from me.

"I'd never hurt an innocent person," I say with a laugh, though my eyes have not yet returned to their usual brown.

"Scythe used to say the same thing," she says, keeping her distance as we walk.

It does disturb me that it's seemingly so easy for one of us to go so bad. I hope that never happens to me. It couldn't right?

I have Tobias and my father, but Scythe had Needle and Sabrina, and he still went bad. But I can't help remembering what Hayyel said.

"You'd never hurt me, Kalana," she told me. "You're out of balance in a good way."

My eyes aren't black anymore. I can feel it before Machete points it out. "Whatever you were just thinking about, keep it in your back pocket for the next time you almost boil over," she says.

"I was thinking of Hayyel."

"Yeah she's nice," Machete says, but it sounds forced. "I

hate snakes, though, so she's hard to be around." Then she catches herself. "Not that I think Scythe is right about her."

"But doesn't it soothe you to be around her?" I ask, my face probably glowing, but I don't care. "Can't you feel her goodness?"

"I can," Machete says, "But it's still hard for me to separate that from what I *see*. I get the impression that isn't as hard for you. Wasn't one of your best friends in high school a handicapped kid?"

My hearts feels like its being squeezed with a fist. It's been so long since anyone has mentioned Tobias's brother Billy to me. They all know better. I've never forgotten him, but I got used to others stepping around him: the giant, disabled elephant in the room that I killed five boys from my high school to avenge. I wasn't prepared for someone I never talked to about him, to bring him up.

Machete takes a very large, concerned step backwards.

"I'm so sorry," Machete says, palms up in surrender. "Alex told us about him. He wanted to make sure we never used the 'R' word around you. I think it was mostly aimed at me. I used to use that word to describe things that were shitty as a way to cuss without really cussing. I didn't always realize how terrible that was."

The 'R' word?

Oh. *That* word. I understand now. I'm never been a fan of

that word, but after what I've been through and what I've put others through because of what they did to a loved one who was mentally challenged, Alex had no assurance that I wouldn't just snap and kill anyone who dared to use that unfair, mean, derogatory word.

I wouldn't, but I certainly hate that word so much I'm glad he weeded it from their vocabulary before I got here. Otherwise, I might've never given these people a chance. I would've hated them before I even got to know them, which would've been a shame. They're actually pretty great.

Machete is really uncomfortable with my thoughtful silence, though my eyes aren't black anymore. I decide to let her off the hook.

"Sorry. I didn't know Alex told you about Billy," I say. "But I'm glad. Saves me a sad story."

Fatherly Love

Tobias and I wake to too-hard knocking on our front door at 1 a.m.

I'm not surprised to see my dad through the keyhole, since it was definitely the typical cop knock, but the blood he's covered in is a little concerning.

He doesn't look in any way blood deprived, so I suspect it's someone else's.

Tobias's eyes are huge at seeing my Dad like this. It's a first for him. Not for me.

"What happened?" I breathe.

It turns out Dad found Sabrina a week ago (a mere two days after the funeral) with some good old fashion police work (which is code for he can't tell us how), and didn't tell any of us because there was some "confidential aftermath." I've slowly put together what that means after living with him for years.

He put her and her grandparents in witness protection. He just can't tell us about it, because it would make them less safe. I suspect only the FBI knows their whereabouts now, and that's how it'll stay.

He found her alone in a trashed apartment with blacked-out windows. She was whimpering, strapped into a *Clockwork Orange*-like contraception that pried her eyes open so she could watch violent and grotesque images to brainwash her toward Scythe's insane way of thinking.

Since she's 2, I doubt it worked, but Dad says she never stopped crying, even when he put them on *the bus*.

That really means *the plane*, but again. He can't say.

Tonight, Scythe was spotted in an alley suspiciously near the sheriff's office, so Dad went after him...alone...on foot.

Scythe seemed to have no idea he was there, which made Dad even more suspicious.

Then he sent his bone scythes at Dad's throat, but Dad leaned back just enough to miss them before Scythe retracted them.

"You've got some reflexes, Sheriff."

"What do you want, Scythe?"

"I want to beat you until you tell me where my daughter is."

"I don't know where she is," Dad said, truthfully.

Scythe sent his vectors again, but this time Dad caught them and almost crushed them between his bare hands (despite the fact that they cut deep into his palms) before he yanked them so hard Scythe did a face plant into the concrete.

I would've loved to see Scythe's bloody face when confronted with Dad's brute strength. Dad just describes it as "a bit surprised." I know that's an understatement.

"You're one of *us*," he said in shock, wiping his gushing mouth.

"I wondered how you were connected to Red's Carpets. It's the new girl. The one with the fury and the long vectors. She's *yours* isn't she?

Dad did not confirm or deny the statement.

"Well, since you took my daughter. I'll just take yours."

That's when Dad felt his eyes darken, and he boiled over.

He started beating Scythe bloody. His bone clubs even came out, which hasn't happened since he beat my mother's killer to death two years ago.

Then he completely blacked out. When he woke, he was lying on his back, covered in Scythe's blood, but Scythe was nowhere in sight.

So he came here, to make sure I was okay.

"He hasn't come here," Tobias assures him.

"I doubt he could get very far after a beating like that," I say. "Are you sure he didn't just crawl somewhere and die?"

"I am," Dad says. "He's a big guy, Kalana. And he had me on the ropes before I blacked out. I don't know how I fought him off."

I do. When my Dad's true rage comes out, he's unstoppable, but the way he's looking at me right now makes me wonder if this time he isn't just being modest.

He really looks worried. It isn't an expression I'm used to seeing on him.

"So...can I sleep on your couch?" Dad asks, but it's not a question. He's going to do it no matter what I say.

I nod.

Old friend

The next week is pretty quiet. Dad takes a leave of absence from work and accompanies me to Red's Carpets every day. The group is excited to "have him back," though he insists it's temporary. But he does train with us and puts everyone to shame every time he beats a demon down. One day, he even somehow manages to break ones back over his knee.

Dr. Menzer even insists on "checking on his patient," even though Dad insists he's just visiting.

I realize he's training so hard for Scythe. He really thinks he's the only thing standing in the way of Scythe killing me. I wish he'd realize I'm not so fragile.

I kill demons for a living! Machete and I took down a demon ourselves the other night during a routine sweep of the city.

Dad continues to sleep on our couch each night, but to "earn his keep" he makes Tobias and us dinner each evening after buying all the groceries too, which makes our week, outside work, pretty easy.

He's actually eating dinner when there's a rough knock at the door. Dad flies to the door and looks through the keyhole. Then he rips the door open to an empty hallway.

The only thing there is a manila envelope.

Dad picks it off the floor and cautiously pulls out the big slick photographs inside.

His face falls. After a deep, sad sigh he hands the pictures to me. Tobias looks over my shoulder as I flip through them.

Who the pictures are of, gagged with silver duct tape, mascara tears and clumps of food in her otherwise perfectly blonde hair, is horrifying.

It's Morgan, my best friend. Who married Eddie Sherman and stayed in our hometown of Haven, Texas.

When I flip over one of the photos, there's an address on the back and a note scribbled in sloppy handwriting that says, "Come alone. Bring the sheriff, and she's dead." He's trying to draw me in, and he picked the perfect thing.

"He has *Morgan*?" Tobias asks with total shock. "How does he have *Morgan*?"

"He's done enough digging to know who I care about," I say. But it confuses me that he didn't just grab Tobias. But I guess Tobias is either in the ER, surrounded by hundreds of people, or here with me. He's protected.

Morgan spends her days at home with the toddler while Eddie works.

"I'm gonna call Eddie," Tobias says, before leaving the

room in pursuit of his smartphone.

Dad doesn't bother telling me not to go. He knows I have no choice. And he wouldn't risk Morgan's life by coming along. He cares about Morgan too. She's like a second daughter to him.

"He's fast," Dad says. "And strong. This isn't going to be easy." He swallows hard. "I'm sorry I brought this on you—"

"By what? Saving a 2-year-old girl from being brainwashed and abused by a psycho?" I ask. "I'm not."

It's true. But I never thought I'd have to face Scythe alone. I never thought he'd have any specific interest in me, though I do want very badly to kill him, for the two unjustified murders I've seen him commit, especially Nee—*Jennifer*.

She didn't deserve that for loving him. She didn't deserve that for daring to disagree with his demented way of seeing the world. She didn't deserve to have her daughter stolen from her grandparents and mentally tortured.

I head on foot toward the address, dressed in my blackest, most covering training suit. Not that I can really be stealthy right now. He knows I'm coming.

I open the door to the apartment address without knocking and carefully creek the door open.

The room's lit with a bare bulb directly above where Morgan sits in the center of the light, conscious and seemingly unhurt.

Since she's gagged with duct tape, all she can do is make mumbled, indiscernible sounds, but they all sound pretty distressed. She's probably trying to tell me it's a trap.

But I already know that.

It's nice to know that my vectors can come out whole seconds faster since they don't have to rip through the flesh of my forearms.

He may be quick with his, but so am I, and mine are longer.

And he doesn't know how furious he's made me by taking Morgan. Sweet, innocent Morgan who has nothing to do with this, outside of the fact that she dared to be my only true friend in high school, aside from Tobias and Billy, of course.

But once I rip the duct tape off of Morgan's mouth, causing a gasp of pain and a rectangular red mark encasing her lips, something hits me hard in the back of the head, and then...nothing.

Images

When I'm conscious again, my eyes are pried open with these uncomfortable, metal contraptions, and I can't move any part of my body, even my neck to look down at myself.

But I can feel the thick shackles around my wrists. They stretch from elbow to wrist and completely block my vectors from coming out. There are also chains wrapped around my waist and many straps and buckles limiting the movement of various parts of my body, like the straps keeping my head perfectly in place and perfectly angled to see the disturbing images projected on the sheet hanging from the ceiling.

They're of various innocent things being beaten to death.

I'm furious he showed these horrific things to his 2-year-old daughter. I'm sure they made her equally as sick, even if she didn't fully understand them.

Then he shows me something shocking.

It's Hayyel and all her "babies" being murdered in excruciating detail. It must've been recent, because I visited her a couple of days ago.

I'll spare you, but it's sickening.

Hayyel.

She was the most innocent soul I had ever encountered,

and I have to see her ripped apart. Her gorgeous blue eyes plucked out.

Vomit constantly gushes from my mouth. The constant burn of acid in my throat becomes more painful by the second.

I don't know what he thinks showing these images will do to me, aside from make me hate him.

He's a monster. He's not convincing me of his insane argument. That it's okay to kill things that aren't pretty. That *that's* how you judge. All the, no doubt, innocent things he's showing me have one thing in common. They're not pretty. They're missing an eye, or a leg, or they just aren't fortunate to be a pretty version of whatever they are.

It's ridiculous. How does he not know how off he is? He's one of us. Why can't he feel the evil he's doing? Why can't he feel the difference between that and how he *should* be? How did he get this way?

At one point in the hours of hell and wetting myself in this chair prison, he appears in my eye line, leaning in from the seams of what I can't see to interrupt his "show."

"How you doing, Kalana?" he asks. "Are you starting to see my vision?"

Absolutely not.

"Yes," I say, failing to sound convincing. "Why don't you unchain me, and we can talk about it?"

I know he won't believe such a quick transformation, but I have to try anything to get out of this chair.

"You don't see it now, but you will."

Then he's gone from my view again and the images continue.

I learn to look at the very top of the screen and blur my eyes a little so I don't have to absorb the disgusting images. I do this for hours. I lose track of time. It's like I'm asleep with my eyes open.

You'd think he'd notice this, but he doesn't. Or he doesn't care. Eventually the sounds of things dying become worse than the images, because what I can imagine is so much worse.

But it's only going to be a matter of time before my vectors break these strange shackles that stretch elbow to wrist.

I closed the fans into a point hours ago and have been slowly drilling through the metal.

Eventually I'll break through.

Hayyel

Though I'm almost free, using my vectors to drill through metal for so long exhausts me, so I pass out. I quickly have a horrible dream that feels real.

It's as if I'm walking into Hayyel's room and discovering her dead.

The glass is broken. The pretty animals remain, clumped together in the corner shaking and traumatized, while the other, less-pretty animals are bloody smears on the floor.

I can see things I've never noticed before. Things on high shelves I've never noticed, stains in top corners of the room that I can't usually see.

Am I taller?

"Sheriff," a voice in my head says. It's Hayyel. She's a broken mess on the floor, lying in a pool of her own black blood, with her beautiful blue eyes missing, but she's breathing. She's not dead.

"I knew you'd come visit me one last time, unfortunately right at this moment."

If Hayyel's alive, is this real? Is Hayyel communicating with me while I sleep? Is she showing me the world through my father's eyes?

"I'm so sorry, Hayyel," booms Dad's voice. "We don't know how he got in." It sounds different from inside his head. Deeper yet more vulnerable at the same time. This is a strange place to listen from.

He stoops beside her and extends his hand, but he's reluctant to touch her. He's not sure where to touch her to comfort her without hurting her. He ends up touching her forehead gently.

Hayyel gasps in pain but tries to suppress it.

Dad quickly removes his hand.

"He has Kalana," Hayyel says.

"I know," Dad says with a sad sigh. I've never heard him sound so devastated. It breaks my heart.

"I know where she is," she says.

I wake with a jerk.

She said "visit me one last time" to my dad, which means he's been there before. I had no knowledge of them ever meeting. That's when I realize, Hayyel must've been the anonymous source that tipped him off about where Scythe held his daughter after he kidnaped her. That's why Scythe tried to kill Hayyel before he took me, so she couldn't tell anyone where he moved me.

Hayyel's psychic abilities stretch further than I thought. If she showed me that in real time, I suspect Dad will get here in 30 minutes or less (if we're still inside the city), so I stay quiet and suffer through more horrific images and sounds, even when Scythe comes to check on my progress about 20 minutes later.

"So how are we doing?" Scythe asks, standing close to me, which is good. He doesn't know that there's only a thin layer of metal between my vectors and him, which I can easily break through to cut his throat.

I'm about to do it when the door gets kicked in, and the dank apartment gets flooded with cops, led by Dad.

I push my vectors through just as he rushes toward Dad and the eight or so cops with no fear. I miss his neck by half an inch.

And I have to cut through all my restraints, before I can get between him and Dad.

I cut away the rest of my shackles first then lift the horrible, tortuous head gear from my face. The metal of the contraception cuts my eyelids a bit on the way off, since I'm rushing.

I free my eyes just in time to see Scythe's vectors launch right at the center of Dad's chest.

Panicked, I stand too quickly and get caught by all the chains wrapping around both me and the chair. I cut through those as well.

Dad whips out his billy club vectors with a spray of blood. I'm shocked to see him do this in front of his men (half look very shocked...half really don't), but I guess he feels he doesn't have a choice. They're the only things keeping Scythe from stabbing him through.

I aim my vectors between Scythe's shoulder blades, where I believe his heart will be if I rip through his back, but something metal blocks me. He's wearing body armor. Of course he is.

He throws the officers that descend on him like they're cardboard cutouts and continues his attack on Dad.

Instead of trying to go through the body armor, I get close enough to embrace him with my vectors instead and try to yank him back.

But he breaks away easily. He's very heavy. It's one thing to cut through something. You just need something very sharp. It's another to lift it. I don't have the same strength as Dad. He could lift this guy if he wanted.

Dad. He's really struggling. Scythe's vectors are slicing the air at him every second. He's barely whipping away these attacks with his bloody bone clubs.

Each swing of his built-in clubs seems slower too. He's in

trouble, and I can't do much against Scythe's body armor.

Scythe has backed him out the door and into the hallway so me (and the cops) have to wait until they're not blocking the doorway to follow.

I rush into the hall just in time to see Dad on one knee, panting, with one blood-stained club raised protectively above his head before a bone-scythe stabs into his chest and rips out his heart.

I scream as I feel that familiar hot, sick feeling I haven't felt since the flight here.

Rage blackout, epic

I wake inside a jail cell, from what feels like a Scythe-homemade-horror film. I'm covered in other people's blood, while an audience of policeman gawk at me like I'm a fascinating, but deadly, zoo animal.

I'm told—by the mere three policemen who survived the Scythe encounter and somehow got me in here—that I blacked out and went on some kind of killing bender as I attempted to chase Scythe across the city on foot.

I lost him fast, but anyone I walked by that hour who was out of balance in a bad way, got shredded.

And I mean shredded. I didn't care who saw. Exposed and surrounded by people, I turned each of them into bloody mulch without so much as a flinch.

One of the policemen asks me if I remember anything. I lie and say no.

I do. For a few minutes, I feel like I'm back in Scythe's apartment with the blacked out windows, watching atrocities projected onto a dirty, torn sheet hanging from the ceiling. Like I didn't commit these despicable acts. But I did.

After cradling my already dead father in my arms and scream-crying as the blood from his gorged chest pooled on the floor around us, I ran out into the streets.

It only takes two blocks to find two gang members who are about to have their way with some poor girl at the dead end of an alley.

They are *probably* going to kill her after, but they aren't murderers yet. That's always stopped me in the past. I've only ever punished *actual* murder, not deterred people permanently before they even committed one.

I agree the second one could be useful in some situations, but it's just not my way.

They have a little bit of goodness in them. A little. One is a father who cares deeply for his three-year-old son despite his inability to see women as people. He probably won't go through with killing her (though he might stand by and let it happen). But the point is, he feels the wrong there. But I snuff out the glimmer of goodness in him without so much as a thought.

It's not that I think that's wrong exactly. I just wish I had stopped and wondered about it at least.

But there is no thinking involved in these decisions.

I just cover the poor girl in their blood and walk off.

Normally, I would've wounded them and stayed with her almost until the police arrived. Comforted her.

But I just leave her—heaving and shocked—in a pool of their slightly differing shades of red, swirled together.

A few blocks later I happen on a typical, armed mugging.

The man tries to protect his wife's purse, and he and the mugger struggle for the gun and the mugger wins.

He's about to shoot them both—this time I'm sure of his intent—and I stab him from behind through his heart before he can fire.

He goes limp and drops the gun before I start tearing him apart, even though he didn't actually kill anyone, as the terrified couple flees.

The last one I kill is a woman who hits her young son in the face with a closed fist every time he shrinks from her too familiar touch.

I can feel what's happening there in private and it disgusts me, so I turn her into a disgusting pile before her traumatized son and the other people on the street before I, again, just leave.

I killed them all, though none of them were technically murderers. They were each bad, but I feel like each one wasn't my call to make. Each one wasn't my place to judge. I deal with absolute murderers, not these gray areas.

But they did all have one thing in common. They were

ugly. Each of them was almost inhumanely ugly. Was it just a coincidence that they were also bad people?

Or did I just kill things because they weren't pretty?

What did Scythe do to me?

Judgement

I wake to Morgan on the other side of the bars, looking at me with worry and fear.

The police were kind enough to spray me with a hose through the bars, but there are still blood stains all over me and circling the drain in the middle of the floor.

I'm sure I look pretty threatening.

It's not like Morgan's never seen me covered in blood before. (I blacked out and killed two guys that were trying to rape her once, who also happened to be two of the five guys that helped murder my friend Billy, Tobias's brother.)

But I can tell this is different. They must've told her about the victims.

They're probably most concerned about the last one: the seemingly blameless mom with her son. They don't know that she was a pedophile.

And telling them now wouldn't help. They think I'm a murderer. This time I agree.

"Did he hurt you?" I ask Morgan through the bars.

"No," says her soft, fluttery voice. "He was actually strangely nice. It was creepy."

I'm not surprised by that, considering how pretty Morgan

is. The flip side of condemning ugly things is that he, apparently, treats pretty things kindly.

I'm actually surprised he let her go. "How did you get away from him?" I ask.

"After he knocked you out, he blindfolded me and left me in an alley. It didn't take long for...*your Dad* to find me."

Dad.

I let out a cry without realizing it at first, but when Morgan tears up, I know that what I saw was real: Scythe ripping out Dad's heart. I'd hoped I wasn't. But it happened. He's dead. Scythe killed him. And I completely lost it.

"I'm sorry, Kalana," Morgan says, voice shaking.

A metal door opens, and Tobias walks through it. Morgan leaves without a word, and Tobias approaches the bars with his eyes filled with tears. He's off-balance with his hair wild, like he hasn't slept since Scythe took me. I wonder how long he had me.

"Are you okay?" he asks me, so much concern in his voice it hurts. I don't deserve his concern anymore.

I don't approach the bars. I want to touch his hand, or any part of him, but I'm afraid he's not safe with me anymore. No one is. Scythe broke me.

"No," I say simply. "Scythe messed with my head." But that

doesn't even begin to explain it. I'm not sure I want to tell Tobias. I don't want to burden him with the details.

"I heard about the woman with her child," he says quickly, seeming to regret it as he says it, but I get it. He has to know the reason behind that. I'd want to know too.

"She was abusing him," I say, trying not to look at his expression when I say it, but I crack and look. His expression, and his whole body, relaxes.

"I figured it had to be something like that," he says, sounding relieved. "And the guy with the gun and the gang bangers. It's easy to guess what they were up to."

"None of them killed anyone, Tobias," I say. "None. I killed people *who hadn't killed anyone*."

I've never realized before how much that distinction matters to me, but it does. It's my calling to kill murderers. That's it. The rest is for someone else to judge. Not me.

"Yeah, but the guy with the gun was probably going to kill *someone*."

"Maybe not." He probably was, but the point is, he didn't.

"And those gang bangers you saved that girl from. I overheard her statement to the police. She said you saved her life."

"I could've saved her without killing them," I say. "It

would've been easy."

"Your Dad had just been killed," he says. "You weren't in a good place." He's always excusing me. Love is certainly blinding sometimes.

"It's not my place to decide who lives or dies based on what someone *might* do."

"That pedophile probably wasn't going to change."

"We don't know that, and even if we did, that doesn't mean she deserved to die."

"I don't know, Kalana," he says. "There's a special place in hell for people who hurt children."

"I agree, but you'd never take someone out for that."

"Because it's not my job."

"Exactly," I practically spit. "Mine either."

He finally stops trying to make it okay. He understands that he can't rationalize this. "So you slipped once," he shrugs. But this isn't something you shrug about.

"*Four* times." There were four of them. "What if I slip again?"

"You won't," he says. "I trust you."

"But I no longer trust myself."

"So what do we do now?" he asks me, looking panicked

about what I might say, but he has to know.

I'm not even sure what I'm going to say until I say it. "I'm going to stay here, and you're going to leave."

"Fine. I'll go home until you come to your senses."

"No," I say, voice shaking. "You're going to leave me."

His eyes flash with anger, which is a rare thing to see in Tobias. I've deeply offended him. I don't think that's ever happened before.

"I. Am. Not," he insists, livid. I've never seen him like this.

"I'm not good enough for you anymore," I say. "I'm not sure I ever was. I wasn't even sure when I avenged your brother's death. That never really felt right to me. But I'm positive I'm not good enough for you now."

"That's not for you to decide," he says.

"Well, I'm doing it anyway," I say. "You have a blind spot when it comes to me."

"Because I love you!"

"Well...you shouldn't. On a good day, I just kill murderers, but that makes me one too."

"But you're an *angel*," he says. "You think I haven't been listening to the strange stories you've been bringing home? You've been entrusted with this mission. I believe that."

"And I've failed. I don't deserve someone like you in my life anymore."

"I don't agree."

"It doesn't matter."

Tobias can tell it's useless to argue any further. He just walks out and doesn't look back. I vainly hope he's going home to pack and move out, but I know he won't leave.

He's just giving me space. He'll come back and keep coming back. And every time I tell him to leave, it'll hurt that much more.

But I'm not going to change my mind. I love him too, and I'll do anything to protect him. That includes saying goodbye.

Jailbreak

A few days later, Alex follows behind a policemen as he unlocks the jail cell and swings open the door.

They leave it that way, expectantly.

I suspect it means Red's Carpets paid off anyone who saw anything, once again sweeping something awful I did under the rug.

"I'm not leaving," I say. "I deserve to be here."

Something strange flashes in Alex's eyes. Something mischievous. I'm afraid of what he's about to say.

"Oh I'm not cleaning up your mess this time," Alex says. "If you think you're no different than a murderer. Fine. I guess we have no choice but to put you with the other murderers."

Oh god. He can't mean—

"There's a whole wing devoted to them at New Orleans prison. I've always wanted to get one of my people in there. Now I finally have an excuse."

"Alex, no," I say. "I'll kill them all."

"Is that a bad thing?"

I don't know anymore. "But I'm unstable right now," I insist. "What if I clean out the entire prison?"

"You won't, Kalana. That's what I'm trying to tell you. You

know the difference between right and wrong."

"I didn't last night."

"You went through an extreme trauma after being brain washed," he dares to say with a shrug. "So you were affected, and you snapped. It's temporary."

"What if it's not?"

"Well, that's what we're going to find out in a prison instead of out on the street. You want to be rehabilitated after what Scythe did to you? Fine. I'll rehabilitate you."

It sounds like a threat and I don't like it. I wonder if Tobias knows about this. I know he couldn't.

What the hell has gotten into Alex?

"You'll only kill the murderers, Kalana. I'm certain of that," he says. "I'm willing to bet on it."

I'm not.

Sept. 13, 2016
Number of Inmates in Local Prison Cut in Half Overnight
By Alice Chase

NEW ORLEANS—Today the number of inmates at New Orleans Penitentiary was suddenly reduced by half.

Last night almost 6,000 prisoners went to sleep, but less than 3,000 woke up when the sun rose.

And no one who remained apparently saw *anything*, including inmates, wardens and janitors.

In fact, many of those questioned, some without even being asked, claimed that they "didn't see anything."

New Orleans officials say they are perplexed and alarmed by this mass exodus of the prison's deadliest offenders.

That's right. 100 percent of the vanished inmates were confirmed murderers.

Yet the newly-appointed Orleans Parish Sheriff, Alex Michaels (who replaced the late Robert Janus), said he isn't concerned about an influx of convicted felons into New Orleans.

"We have reason to believe that this is a prison break, and escaped convicts tend to get as far away from where they were being held as possible to avoid re-arrest."

Sheriff Michaels was also not confident of recapturing these criminals.

"We unfortunately have very few leads," he said. "But the good news is, taxpayers will no longer have to pay to house and feed convicted murders."

Sheriff Michaels smiled when he said that.

The Reporter

"Alice," breathes my boss calmly when I answer the phone on my desk, but I know what's about to happen isn't going to be pleasant.

Shit. Shit. Shit.

"Yes?" I ask weakly into the phone.

"Come see me."

Then he hangs up.

I hyperventilate. I grope for the bottle of Xanax in my purse, but let it go as soon as I find it. It would seem strange if halfway through the meeting I was suddenly very calm. He wouldn't think I was taking this seriously. But I take my career very seriously, and I'm pretty sure I just ended it.

I shake as I walk through the door of his office.

"Close the door," he orders.

I do and almost convulse as I perch on the chair before his desk, ankles crossed, trying to look as small and lady-like as possible. Maybe he'll take pity on me.

He has the article printed before him. Of course he does.

The last line is circled in thick, red marker.

His expression is stern and unforgiving.

"Why is this sentence here?" he asks in a hard voice.

"Which one?" I stall. I know which one.

The one that says, "Sheriff Michaels smiled when he said that."

I swallow. "It was in my original draft," I say, knowing it's the worst defense ever. It also got *crossed out* of my first draft when it was submitted to him, my editor, as a PDF. And I remember exactly what he wrote in the little comment bubble beside it:

"Let's not make assumptions about facial expressions. Some people smile when they're nervous. Some people look like they're smiling when they're not. Even if he did smile, ending on this statement puts too much emphasis on this quote. I'm overjoyed that he gave us this quote, so let's not hammer him into the ground for it."

"We discussed that your article would end on a quote," he says, his voice growing hotter and angrier with each word. "Did you forget?"

I've learned quickly that lying gets you nowhere in this business.

"No," I admit.

"So what happened?"

"I put it back in before I published it on the website," I say, voice shaking. "But I can just as easily take it out."

"It's too late for that," he says, looking not remotely comforted by my weak-sauce solution. "It's already out there. I've already gotten three calls about it."

So that's how he knew it was there. He never reads our website. He should, since he's the editor, but he never does. Once something is out of his hands, he doesn't worry about it anymore. That's why I thought I could get away with it. Not that I've ever attempted anything so stupid before. Why did I do something so stupid?

Because it's the truth. He smiled. I almost wrote, "Sheriff Michaels smiled a little when he said that..." to try and soften it, but it wasn't accurate. He didn't smile a little. He smiled a lot. I could've even described it as a grin, but I knew enough not to throw that word around. I wish I had known better than throwing that whole sentence around. He told me not to include it, but I ignored him.

"This is certainly a fireable offense," he tells me. He doesn't have to tell me. I know I'm about to be sent to HR.

I try to keep myself from nodding in agreement. I concentrate on keeping my chin even and my expression impassive, but I'm sure I look terrified.

"But I'm not going to do that," he says with a sigh. Then his whole body relaxes, and he puts the printout aside.

What?

"I have a better idea."

I hold my breath. I'm not sure what he's about to say will be any better.

"You want to be an investigative reporter?" he asks.

I don't, actually. Those people get killed. I've seen *House of Cards*. I just have to tell the truth when I write. But if this opening leads to not getting fired, I have to take it. I nod.

"Good," he says with a smile tugging on one side of his mouth. "I need you to investigate this woman."

Then he holds up a color printout of a picture that was clearly taken on someone's smartphone. The subject is a woman wearing an orange prison jumper, sitting on a prison cot, covered in blood.

I mean really covered in thick, wet blood from head to toe. And I notice something else. Her wrists are covered in these long, white cat skin gloves. Strange accessory for prison, especially since they don't have a drop of blood on them.

I barely recognized her, but I do.

"Kalana Janus?" I ask.

His expression falls like a mask. I think because he's not sure if he should smile or continue to look stern, so he just goes blank.

"*Janus?*" he says, like the name is alien. "I've heard her last name is *Engel.*"

"Her maiden name is Janus," I say. "She's the late sheriff's daughter, but they don't admit that publicly."

His mouth gapes. "How do you know that?" he demands.

"The AP story about the plane with the redacted terrorist attack a few months ago," I say. "I wrote it. She was the one on the plane who got carried off, covered in blood, allegedly because of 'ruptured wrists.' I just wasn't allowed to say so." Because she was undergoing medical treatment at press time.

The shock on his face gives way to admiration. It's unexpected.

"Write me a story that exposes how she's connected to the disappearances on the plane and the prison, and I won't fire you," he grins as he says. It's absolutely a grin.

Shit.

Kalana Janus, whoever she is, is going to personally murder me. But I can't get fired in this economy. My career would never recover. So I take a deep breath and say...

"Done."

www.ingramcontent.com/pod-product-compliance
Lightning Source LLC
Chambersburg PA
CBHW070637130626
46555CB00006B/2591